To Jonathan,
may all your dreams come true.
Mom

To my parents, who encouraged
my passion for art.
Joe

Acknowledgments

The author wishes to thank Joe Rossi
for his light-hearted illustrations,
and Mark J. Price, whose February 19th 2007
Akron Beacon Journal article about
Ariel Bradley was the inspiration for this book.
And, of course Vanita Oelschlager.

Ariel Bradley

SPY for GENERAL WASHINGTON

★

WRITTEN BY
Lynda Durrant

ART BY
Joe Rossi

VanitaBooks, LLC

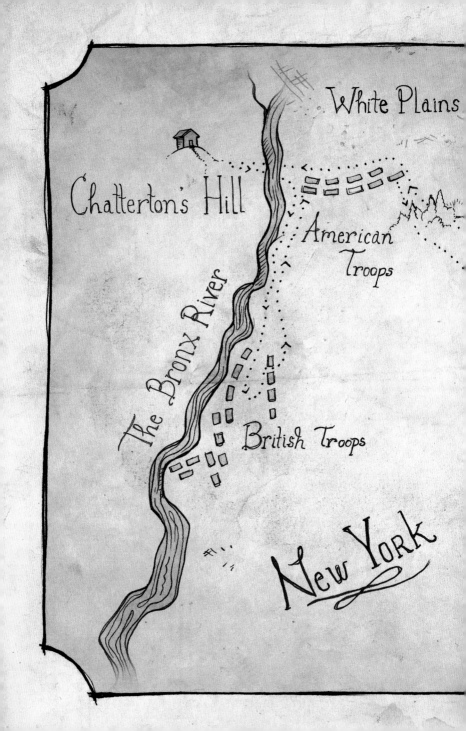

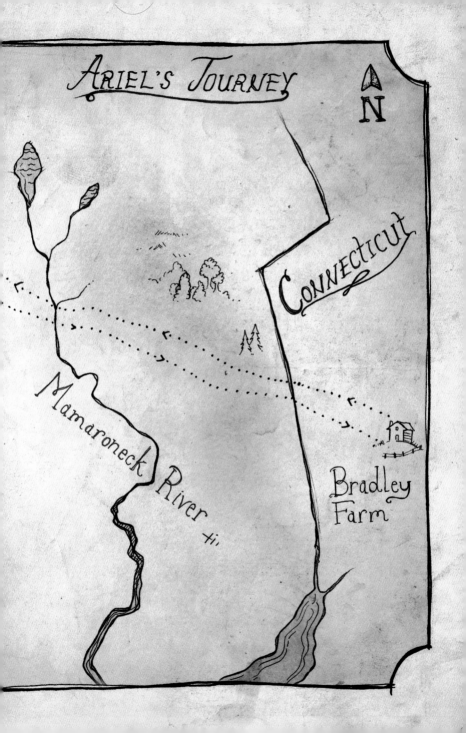

CHAPTER ONE
Cobbler

Nine-year-old Ariel Bradley stood tall as a soldier. It was late October 1776 on his father's farm in Connecticut, and the warm weather lingered. The oaks, maples, elms, beeches, and sycamores blazed still with autumn reds, yellows, oranges, plums, and golds.

Ariel's mouth watered, for Ma was baking a cobbler. As it baked, the delicious scents of blueberries, raspberries, black raspberries, butter, molasses, and cinnamon-sugar steamed right into his nose.

Ma took the cobbler from the oven of the summer kitchen. It was evenly browned with thick, purple fruit syrup bubbling around the edges. No one made cobbler as good as Ariel's mother.

"Ma, may I have a bowl of cobbler now, while it's still warm?"

Ma replied, "I've been saving the summer berries in the icehouse. I've saved the best cream from the dairy. You know I'm saving the cobbler for when your brothers come home."

Ariel stood taller still.

His brothers, Thaddeus and James—soldiers in General Washington's Continental Army—were coming home today on soldier's leave. Ariel wondered why his brothers were coming home. Surely they were bringing good news?

CHAPTER TWO
Soldier's Leave

As the sun was setting, Thaddeus and James Bradley walked up the Old Post Road. How the brass buttons on their uniforms sparkled!

Ariel met them at the farm gate.

James smiled at his little brother.

Thaddeus laughed. "We're looking forward to Ma's good cooking. Does she know we're coming? Did she get word?"

"She made a basin of cobbler," Ariel returned. "She saved the best cream, cold in the icehouse."

Thaddeus laughed again. "She got word."

That evening, the seven Bradleys sat around the dinner table. On the sideboard were the cobbler, bowls and spoons, and a pitcher of the best cream.

"How goes the war?" their father asked softly.

Eldest brother Thaddeus looked up from his turkey and sweet potatoes. "General Washington's army has the bravest soldiers the world has ever known."

Mr. Bradley scowled. "The bravest soldiers in the world lost the Battle of Long Island."

Thaddeus shouted, "Because the British have their redcoats, thousands of them! King George III has hired regiments of Hessians to fight for him. The Yeager regiments wear dark green coats, all the better to hide in the forests."

"In German, Yeager means 'hunter'," Ariel whispered to his little sisters.

James spoke up. "The British have more muskets, more gunpowder, more food, and more horses; more of everything.

"The king's general, General Howe, is marching his men north toward the little town of White Plains, New York. The woods are thick in New

York, and the enemy camps are well guarded. We don't know how many men he has."

Thaddeus and James looked at Ariel. Thaddeus said, "General Washington has a plan we'd like to talk about after the small fry are a-bed."

Mr. Bradley looked down the table. "To bed, then. Mrs. Bradley, prepare the little ones."

Ariel cried out, "The cobbler! Pa!"

His little sisters began to cry.

"They must have their cobblers first, Mr. Bradley." Quickly, Ma spooned cobbler into bowls. She poured thick golden cream over each.

Ariel took a big bite. His cobbler was no longer warm, but this war was not going well, and his brothers and General Washington's men were so brave.

He could eat cold cobbler.

CHAPTER THREE

"Can you act the Johnny Raw?"

The next morning, James asked Ariel, "General Washington wants to know, can you act the Johnny Raw?"

"The Johnny Raw?" Ariel echoed.

"The Johnny Raw; can you act the perfect country bumpkin?"

Ariel looked to James, to Thaddeus, in perfect confusion.

"Mark that face," Thaddeus said, "and remember it. That's the country bumpkin face we need."

Pa said, "You may borrow Salt. She's a Johnny Raw horse." He put his hand on Ariel's head. "Good luck, my son."

A tearful Ma hugged him.

Ariel asked, "Where am I going? Who is Johnny Raw?"

"Mark that face and remember it," Thaddeus repeated. "Act the Johnny Raw, and see what you will."

Salt was the old white mare that stood a-pasture. She'd worked the Bradley farm for years and had earned her rest.

Thaddeus tied a rope around Salt's neck. James slung a bag of dried corn over Ariel's shoulders.

Salt dug her hooves into the soft grass. The brothers pulled and pulled. Finally, she stepped stiff-legged onto the Old Post Road. Her head dipped low.

"We'll tell you how along the way." Thaddeus said softly to Ariel, "You're to be a spy for General Washington."

Ariel's mouth dropped open. "A spy?"

"White Plains is more than 70 miles north

from here. We'll be walking cross country for four days." Thaddeus left the Old Post Road and walked across their neighbor's fallow field. His brothers and Salt followed.

CHAPTER FOUR
Farms and Fields

On the first day, the brothers walked across Connecticut farms and fields. By the second day, they'd crossed the Mamaroneck River and were deep in the New York forests. If General Howe's British army was in New York, his soldiers were well hidden amid the thick stands of pines and hardwoods.

As they walked, Ariel was filled to bursting with questions. Why was he to be a spy? Who was he to spy upon? What was he to learn? How was he to tell General Washington his spy news? How would he return to Ma and Pa?

"But how will I..." he began.

James put his finger to his lips. "The trees have ears," he whispered. "We'll tell you when you need to know."

On the third day, they headed north following the Bronx River, but well away from its banks. By nightfall on the fourth day, they were just north of White Plains.

Thaddeus and James set up camp.

"What if I get scared?" Ariel asked softly.

"You'll not be scared if you do exactly what we tell you to do," James said, softer still. "Go to sleep and tomorrow, see what you will."

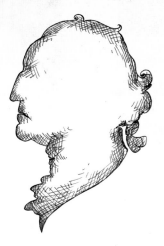

CHAPTER FIVE
General Washington

In the morning, Thaddeus explained General Washington's plan. Speaking softly, he told Ariel what to look for in the enemy camps. "How many soldiers? How many muskets? How many war horses and officers? Our general has great faith in you, Ariel. With your face in perfect confusion, keep

asking about the mill, but look sharp—right, left, right, left—and remember what you see."

Thaddeus lifted Ariel onto Salt's back. James tied the bag of dried corn across Ariel's right shoulder. Thaddeus and James stood back to take a close look at their brother.

Thaddeus said, "A Johnny Raw would not wear shoes." Ariel kicked his shoes to the ground.

James said, "A Johnny Raw would not wear such a grand hat." Ariel tossed his tri-corned hat to James.

Ariel's feet and head felt cold in the late autumn sunshine. "I shall act the Johnny Raw, the perfect country bumpkin. I shall ask again and again about the mill."

"And see what you will," Thaddeus reminded him.

The brothers stepped into the town of White Plains. As a signal, James yipped like a fox.

A small red house perched at the very top of Chatterton's Hill. When a tall man in a dark blue coat stepped out, Ariel gasped. It was General Washington! The general nodded to Ariel.

Ariel raised his right hand in return. He pressed his knees into Salt's sides. "Walk on, old Salt."

CHAPTER SIX

Where's the mill?

He and Salt wandered south, down the east side of the Bronx River.

Soon his heart pounded, for there were Hessians on the riverbank, sitting before a camp fire.

"Guten Morgen," one of the soldiers called out.

"Good morning." Ariel took a deep breath. He marked his face in perfect confusion. "Where's the mill, good sirs?"

Hessians gathered round, arguing in German, and pointing every which way. As they argued, Ariel turned to the right. He turned to the left. He looked every which way. And everywhere he looked, there were Hessians in dark, forest-green uniforms. How many soldiers? How many muskets? How many gunpowder horns? Were their horses well fed and healthy?

Ariel thanked them. "Walk on, old Salt." Salt was tired. With her head down and her eyes almost closed, she softly wheezed.

Old Salt limped as they headed downriver.

Ariel pinched his arm hard as he and Salt

entered the British army camp. Tears, from fear and from pain, welled in his eyes and ran down his cheeks.

"I can't find the mill!" he cried. "Where's the mill, good sir?"

"There's no mill here, boy," an officer replied. He took a-hold of Salt's neck rope and led her toward the tents.

Ariel turned to the right. He turned to the left. He looked every which way. Soldiers in bright red uniforms; thousands of them!

Ariel cried out. "Where's the mill?"

The soldier led Ariel and Salt to the biggest tent. "General Howe? A lad to see you, sir. He says he's looking for a mill."

CHAPTER SEVEN
General Howe

British officers poured out of the tent. Ariel's heart was in his throat. The king's general stood before him!

General Howe was red-faced in anger. "Why are you here?"

"I can't find the mill, good sir!"

"There's no mill on this river, young man, none that I know of," General Howe growled. "Where are you from? Why are you here? What are you really looking for?"

Ariel held up the bag of dried corn and sobbed. "Pa wants this corn ground into cornmeal. He'll be so angry if I don't find the mill!" He turned to the left. He turned to the right. He looked every which way. "Where's the mill, sir?"

General Howe sighed. "Wait here."

Old Salt stretched her skinny neck, opened her mouth wide, and coughed. The officers laughed as they ducked again into General Howe's tent.

A soldier with a musket stood next to Ariel.

Ariel wiped the tears from his eyes. He looked to the right. He looked to the left. He looked every which way: thousands of muskets, thousands of well-fed soldiers, hundreds of horses with shining coats, and tents as far down the riverbank as he could see.

Every time a group of soldiers marched by, Ariel cried out, "Where's the mill, good sirs?"

Finally, General Howe and his officers joined him.

The captain spoke. "The town of White Plains is to the north, upriver about five miles. There might be a mill there." He waved Ariel away.

Ariel felt every soldier staring at him as he and Salt turned away from the army camp. "Walk on, Salt old girl."

CHAPTER EIGHT

"Thank you, Ariel Bradley"

Salt stepped slowly, painfully. She stopped to shudder the dust off her coat, and then limped forward.

Ariel remembered what his brothers had told him to look for. How many soldiers? How many rifles?

How many horses? How many bags of gunpowder and shot? How much food?

Ariel and Salt tottered north, and alongside the Hessian camp. The same Hessians sat around their campfire. "Guten Morgen," they called out.

"Good morning," Ariel replied.

Ariel returned to White Plains. Salt groaned as she trudged slowly up Chatterton's Hill. Out the front door of the little red house stepped General George Washington.

Ariel jumped off Salt's back. His sack of dried corn fell to the ground.

He took a deep breath. "General Washington, I believe there are twice as many British soldiers than Hessians soldiers. Every soldier has a clean musket and a good supply of shot and gunpowder. Plenty of

food, tents, blankets, and extra boots; not a hospital tent in sight; their horses are well fed, too."

General Washington's captain said, "Perhaps two Hessian regiments and four British regiments. That could be 12,000 men, sir. Fresh troops."

General Washington spoke softly. "Twelve thousand fresh troops."

The general looked south, down the Bronx River, as though he could see through the thick canopy of trees to enemy troops camped on its eastern bank. He gazed south for a long time.

Ariel spoke up. "General Washington, sir, my brothers said you told me to act the Johnny Raw. Pa told me that Salt is a Johnny Raw horse."

The captain laughed. "That she is."

General Washington placed his hand on Ariel's head. "Thank you, Ariel Bradley. Thank your brothers when you see them, Thaddeus and James."

"Yes, sir."

Ariel and Salt traveled east, well away from the enemy camps.

CHAPTER NINE
A Soldier's Horse

At the rallying point and out of danger, Ariel leapt off Salt's back. The mare sprawled on the meadow grass. She rolled in the clover.

Ariel called, "James and Thaddeus, I'm here."

His brothers ran from behind the trees.

James shook his hand while Thaddeus whooped and hollered. "We knew you could do it! We knew you could act the Johnny Raw!" he crowed. His brothers handed him his hat and shoes.

Ariel began, "I spoke to General Washington. Twelve thousand British and Hessian soldiers...."

James put his finger to his lips. "The trees have ears," he whispered.

Thaddeus said, "On General Washington's orders, we're to take you and Salt home before we rejoin the battles."

In the golden autumn sunlight, Ariel glowed. He'd acted the Johnny Raw and fooled General Howe and all his men. He'd helped General Washington, his brothers, his family, and his country. He stood tall as a soldier.

"Might Ma make a cobbler just for me?" he asked.

"She might," James returned, "but first things first." James doffed his tri-corner hat. "There's a creek bed yonder. I'll fetch some water for Salt. A soldier takes good care of his horse. She's a soldier's horse now."

"I'll fetch the water," Ariel said.

The End

MORE TO THE STORY...

This book is based on a true event. When Ariel Bradley was just nine years old, General George Washington asked him 'to act the Johnny Raw'—an eighteenth century term for a country bumpkin. On a broken-down horse, with a sack of dried corn over his shoulder, Ariel blundered into the enemy camps, asking directions 'to the mill.'

Ariel took careful account of how many soldiers and how much equipment General William Howe had. His valuable information helped the Americans win the Battle of White Plains, in New York State.

When Ariel became a man, he and his wife and children moved to northern Ohio. Ariel Bradley was the first citizen and founder of Mogadore, Ohio.

Ariel was born in September 1767. He died in 1857, at the age of 90. After his death, the town of Mogadore erected a granite monolith to remember Ariel Bradley's heroism in the American Revolution.

GLOSSARY

Icehouse – before refrigerators, people would cut ice from ponds and store the ice bricks in a small building with thick stone walls. An icehouse kept fresh food cold.

The Battle of Long Island – also called the Battle of Brooklyn, was fought by 10,000 American troops (soldiers) led by General George Washington, against 20,000 British and Hessian troops led by Major-General Lord William Howe and Lieutenant-General Leopold Von Heister, on August 27th 1776. The Americans lost. As the British occupied the City of New York, General Washington marched his troops north toward the town of White Plains.

British redcoats – The British Army dressed in bright red coats.

King George III – this monarch had been the King of Great Britain and the King of Ireland for sixteen years before the Americans declared their independence in July 1776. He died in 1820 as King of the United Kingdoms of Great Britain and Ireland. He was also known as the King who lost America.

Hessians – these were hired soldiers from the German-speaking principalities of Europe. Germany did not become a nation until 1871.

Yeager regiments – these Hessians specialized in forest fighting. Their dark green coats were an early camouflage.

Muskets, gunpowder, and **shots** – muskets look like rifles but they need to be reloaded after every firing. A musket fires a mixture of exploding gunpowder and tiny bullets called shots.

Major-General Lord William Howe – Howe was King George III's uncle. In August 1776, his troops occupied New York City. In September 1777, more of his troops occupied Philadelphia. In April 1778, his nephew allowed him to retire and return to England.

Johnny Raw – an 18th century term for a country bumpkin.

Mill – farmers would take their grain to a miller who would grind the corn, wheat, rye, and oats into flour.

Tri-corned hat – the three-cornered hat was the fashion in the 18th century. Men decorated their tri-corned hats with feathers, ribbons, and silver or gold medals.

Guten morgen – good morning in German.

Granite monolith – a monolith is a free-standing stone, meant as a remembrance.

ABOUT THE AUTHOR

Lynda Durrant has had seven award-winning historic fiction novels for young readers published by Clarion Books. Her local historical society published a novel which takes place in her 1850 farmhouse. She also has e-books published on Kindle. *Ariel Bradley, Spy for General Washington* is her first picture book.

ABOUT THE ILLUSTRATOR

Joe Rossi is an Illustrator and Graphic Designer currently working in Akron, Ohio. Originally from Youngstown, he graduated Cum Laude from Youngstown State University in 2008 with a Bachelor of Fine Arts and a Minor in Art History. He is the recipient of numerous Addy Awards and has had artwork published in the *Official Michael Jackson Opus*, by Kraken Opus. *Ariel Bradley, Spy for General Washington* is his second children's book. His first was *Knees, The Mixed-up World of a Boy With Dyslexia* authored by Vanita Oelschlager.

ABOUT THE ART

When creating art for Ariel Bradley I wanted it to be as rich and inviting as the story itself. This was the first book where I had the opportunity to experiment with color and wanted it to be something special. I'm rather partial to watercolor and instantly knew that the brush strokes could add a much desired depth to the art. First I painted a base layer of color washes and started to outline the edges with illustration pens. I layered this technique many times until I was satisfied. Scanning the art piece by piece I built the final illustrations up, enhancing each one by adding lighting effects, color variations, and paper textures.

The color of the outlines was carefully selected, feeling black would be far too dreary and drain all the life from the page, I chose a rich, dark brown to add warmth to the book. Everything had to feel organic and rustic, from the brown outlines to the aged paper effects, just as rich with history as the story.

The art to me was more about the reader feeling an emotion by looking at each illustration. By using certain hues and tones I wanted the lighting to be a key element and to set the mood to each painting. Warm yellows and oranges were used to capture the essence of an early fall morning. Deep and dark reds helped emphasize General Howe's intimidating presence. And cool blues and purples were painted against a stark white moon to set a chill on a cold autumn night. All of these elements eventually came together to help me flush out the story of a brave, young boy. Hopefully the art strengthens the bond readers feel with Ariel, and help them fall in love with his adventure.

All net profits from this book will
benefit Fisher House Foundation.

Fisher House Foundation, Inc. is a not-for-profit organization
dedicated to helping America's military families in their time of need.
The Foundation builds "comfort homes" at the campuses of major
military and VA hospitals, enabling families to be close to a sick or
injured loved one. Fisher Houses are beautifully decorated homes
with 7 to 21 suites, a common kitchen, laundry facilities, spacious
dining room, and an inviting living room, with library and toys
for children.

Through the generous support of the American public, the
Foundation covers all costs to stay at an Army, Air Force or Navy
Fisher House, (there has never been a charge to stay at a VA Fisher
House). No one pays to stay at a Fisher House. We truly believe
that a family's love is the best medicine!

Fisher House Foundation provides a "home away from home" that
enables America's military families to be close to a loved one during
sickness or injury.